Printed in the United States

10 9 8 7 6 5 4 3 2 1

Green Writers Press is a Vermont-based publisher whose mission is to spread a message of hope and renewal through the words and images we publish. We will adhere to our commitment to preserving and protecting the natural resources of the earth. To that end, a percentage of our proceeds will be donated to environmental and social-justice activist groups. Green Writers Press gratefully acknowledges the generosity of individual donors, friends, and readers to help support the environment and our publishing initiative. For information about funding or getting involved in our publishing program, contact Green Writers Press.

· *Giving Voice to Writers & Artists Who Will Make the World a Better Place*
Green Writers Press | Brattleboro, Vermont
www.greenwriterspress.com

*The illustrations were rendered with colored inks, crayon, watersoluble pencils, and digital techniques.*
*The Spotted Salamander range map is based on data from USGS National Amphibian Atlas, 2014.*
Visit the illustrator's website: msodanoillustration.com  |  Visit the author's website: katyfarber.com

ISBN: 9780999076644

PRINTED ON RECYCLED PAPER BY THOMSON-SHORE.

Manufactured by Thomson-Shore, Dexter, MI (USA); RMA207HC42, February 2018

# Salamander Sky

*by* Katy Farber

*illustrated by* Meg Sodano

I watch the rain
slide down the glass
*pitter, patter*
*drip, drop.*

A flutter in my heart
of hope
that this is the day,
my day to help the salamanders.

I should be getting dressed for school,
brushing my teeth,
stuffing my backpack full,
sliding on my shoes.

But the flutter won't go away
because it's April, the month, my name,
and thousands of salamanders
might cross the roads tonight.

I know this,
my mom, the scientist,
taught me
the story of the spotted salamanders.

They live below the ground
under layers of earth,
snug among the roots,
hidden and secret most of the year.

Waiting, waiting,
for the rain to be just right,
on a few spring nights,
pouring for hours and hours,
coating the world in wetness.

Perfect
for a sopping, slimy,
shy creature
to creep up and out
of its tree-root home
across rumbling roads,
through sopping-wet leaves,
to the pools and ponds
for a spring ball
like no other.

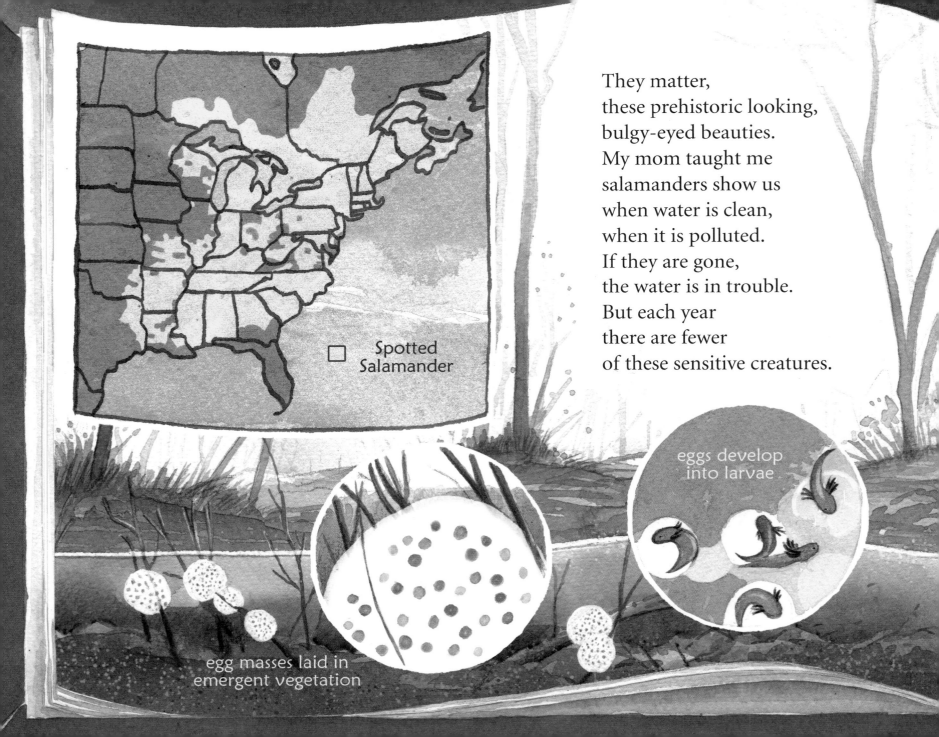

They matter,
these prehistoric looking,
bulgy-eyed beauties.
My mom taught me
salamanders show us
when water is clean,
when it is polluted.
If they are gone,
the water is in trouble.
But each year
there are fewer
of these sensitive creatures.

Spotted
Salamander

eggs develop
into larvae

egg masses laid in
emergent vegetation

They matter
to our woods,
our ponds,
our wetlands,
all connected
to everything that lives here
and everywhere else—
a piece of a puzzle.

aquatic
larvae

terrestrial
adult

These secret creatures matter
but their path is not easy—
pollution,
roads,
buildings,
climate change,
all hurt them.

I want to protect
these quiet
mysterious creatures
who only come out
on a scattering of nights,
maybe tonight,
a night in April,
the month, my name.

The school day crawls on
slowly, like a salamander,
minutes into long hours,
staring at the clock
all I can see
is rain and bright yellow spots.

Home, dinner, homework—
all as rain falls in sheets.
Mom smiles and says,
"Maybe, maybe."

I'm reading in bed,
not sleeping,
waiting,
just like the salamanders.
Finally Mom pokes her head in,
grins, nods.

I pop up from my bed
into loud rain pants,
thick rubber jacket,
squeaky boots—
out into the cool night air.
It is finally here,
my time to help the salamanders.

We walk down the dirt road
*squish, squash, squish,*
rain pelting us sideways.
I feel a chill deep in my bones,
even though I am not cold.

We scan the wet, shiny road
for a four-legged, slow-moving friend
making its way steadily
back to where it started—
the pond and wetlands
where it was born.

Trouble is, the salamanders are slow,
and cars come quick.
Many are hit by people
who drive and don't know
this night is for spotted salamanders.

So we come out to look for them,
to carry them across the road
to where they would safely go
if we didn't drive here.

I sweep my eyes back and forth,
eyelashes dripping—
my mom ahead,
shiny and slick, too.

We are like two ghosts
wandering together
down this dark road,
light from the flashlights
scattering in the rain.

Then I see a long black body,
bright yellow spots,
tiny toes and fingers;
my heart leaps to my throat.
"Mom!" I yell, "I found one!"

When I pick it up
its body is cold and heavy,
its big eyes look up at me.
I carry it across the road,
set it down gently
on the other side.

Deep inside I feel warm.
Even though I am dripping wet,
there is a glow in my chest.
I have done something good.

I turn back and smile at my mom,
rain dripping in my mouth,
and look for more friends to help
cross the road
under this perfect
salamander sky.